Parsnip

A lift-the-flap book by Sue Porter

MATHEW PRICE LIMITED

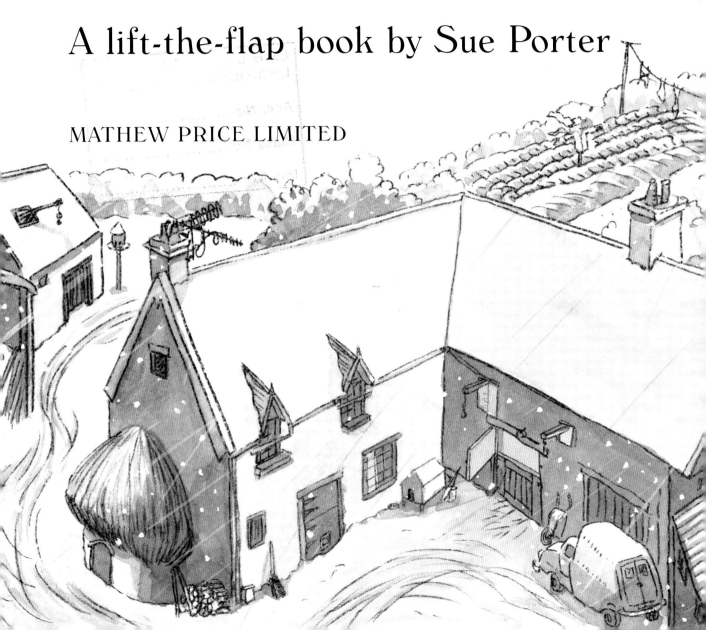

That night, the wind howled and swirled about. But the sheep up on the hill were warm in their woolly coats.

Only Mama's tiny, newborn lamb shivered and lay still.

Gently, Mama carried her baby down to the barn where all the other farm animals slept.

Mama asked the farmer to take her baby into the warm farmhouse.

Now, where could a shivering little lamb be put, to keep warm?

"Not here!"

Aah! The parsnip box was just right.

The little lamb was very still and very quiet.

"She's very still!"

"She's very quiet."

The little lamb
opened her eyes,

wiggled her tail,

stretched her
legs and
stood up.

Champy said he'd help her find her Mama.

First, though, she needed something to keep her warm.

"Oh dear, this is too big . . ."

"... and this is too small."

"Come on," Champy said,
"let's find your Mama now."

But the little lamb had already gone.

The little lamb told Mama all about her new friends and her parsnip-box bed. Mama thought Parsnip would make a lovely name.

"You're my very own little Parsnip," she said, giving her baby a cuddle.

THE END